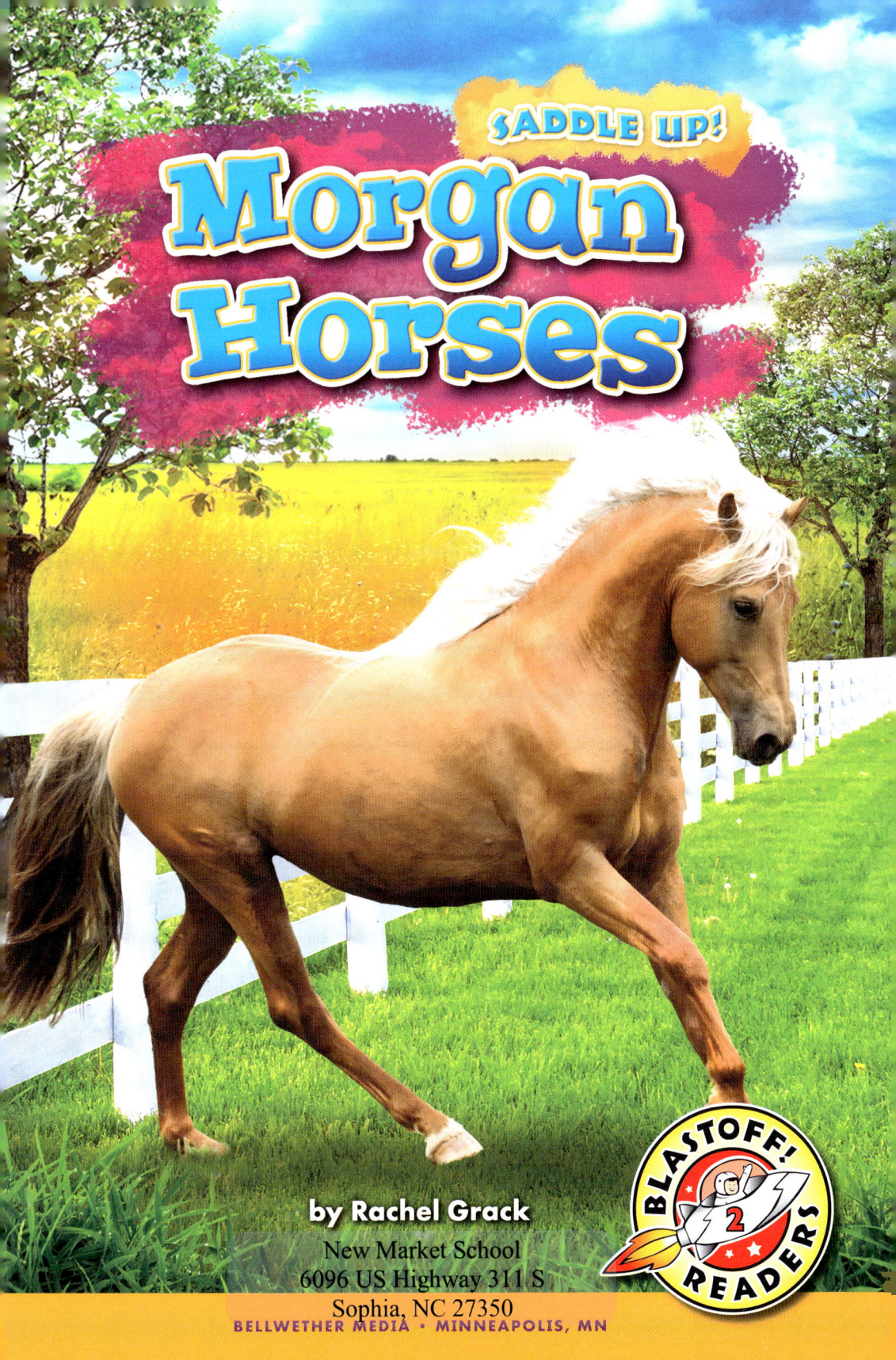

SADDLE UP!
Morgan Horses

by Rachel Grack

New Market School
6096 US Highway 311 S
Sophia, NC 27350

BELLWETHER MEDIA • MINNEAPOLIS, MN

BLASTOFF! READERS 2

Blastoff! Readers are carefully developed by literacy experts to build reading stamina and move students toward fluency by combining standards-based content with developmentally appropriate text.

 **Level 1** provides the most support through repetition of high-frequency words, light text, predictable sentence patterns, and strong visual support.

 **Level 2** offers early readers a bit more challenge through varied sentences, increased text load, and text-supportive special features.

 **Level 3** advances early-fluent readers toward fluency through increased text load, less reliance on photos, advancing concepts, longer sentences, and more complex special features.

★ **Blastoff! Universe**

This edition first published in 2021 by Bellwether Media, Inc.

No part of this publication may be reproduced in whole or in part without written permission of the publisher. For information regarding permission, write to Bellwether Media, Inc., Attention: Permissions Department, 6012 Blue Circle Drive, Minnetonka, MN 55343.

Library of Congress Cataloging-in-Publication Data

Names: Koestler-Grack, Rachel A., 1973- author.
Title: Morgan horses / by Rachel Grack.
Description: Minneapolis, MN : Bellwether Media, Inc., 2021. | Series: Blastoff! readers: saddle up! | Includes bibliographical references and index. | Audience: Ages 5-8 | Audience: Grades K-1 | Summary: "Relevant images match informative text in this introduction to Morgan horses. Intended for students in kindergarten through third grade"– Provided by publisher.
Identifiers: LCCN 2020033243 (print) | LCCN 2020033244 (ebook) | ISBN9781644874301 (library binding) | ISBN 9781648341076 (ebook)
Subjects: LCSH: Morgan horse–Juvenile literature.
Classification: LCC SF293.M8 K64 2021 (print) | LCC SF293.M8 (ebook) | DDC 636.1/77-dc23
LC record available at https://lccn.loc.gov/2020033243
LC ebook record available at https://lccn.loc.gov/2020033244

Text copyright © 2021 by Bellwether Media, Inc. BLASTOFF! READERS and associated logos are trademarks and/or registered trademarks of Bellwether Media, Inc.

Editor: Elizabeth Neuenfeldt   Designer: Laura Sowers

Printed in the United States of America, North Mankato, MN.

Table of Contents

All-American Horses	4
Small but Mighty	6
Morgan Horse Beginnings	12
Talented Friends	16
Glossary	22
To Learn More	23
Index	24

All-American Horses

Morgan horses are a favorite American **breed**. They make excellent work horses. These horses also shine in shows and races.

Morgans stand out in many ways!

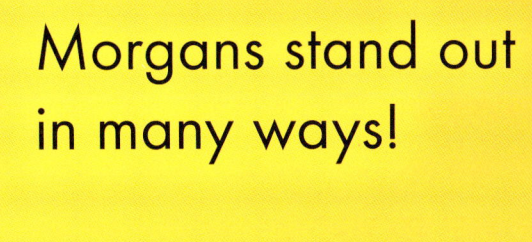

Small but Mighty

Most Morgans stand between 14 and 15 **hands** high.

They are small but powerful. Morgan horses can pull heavy loads with ease.

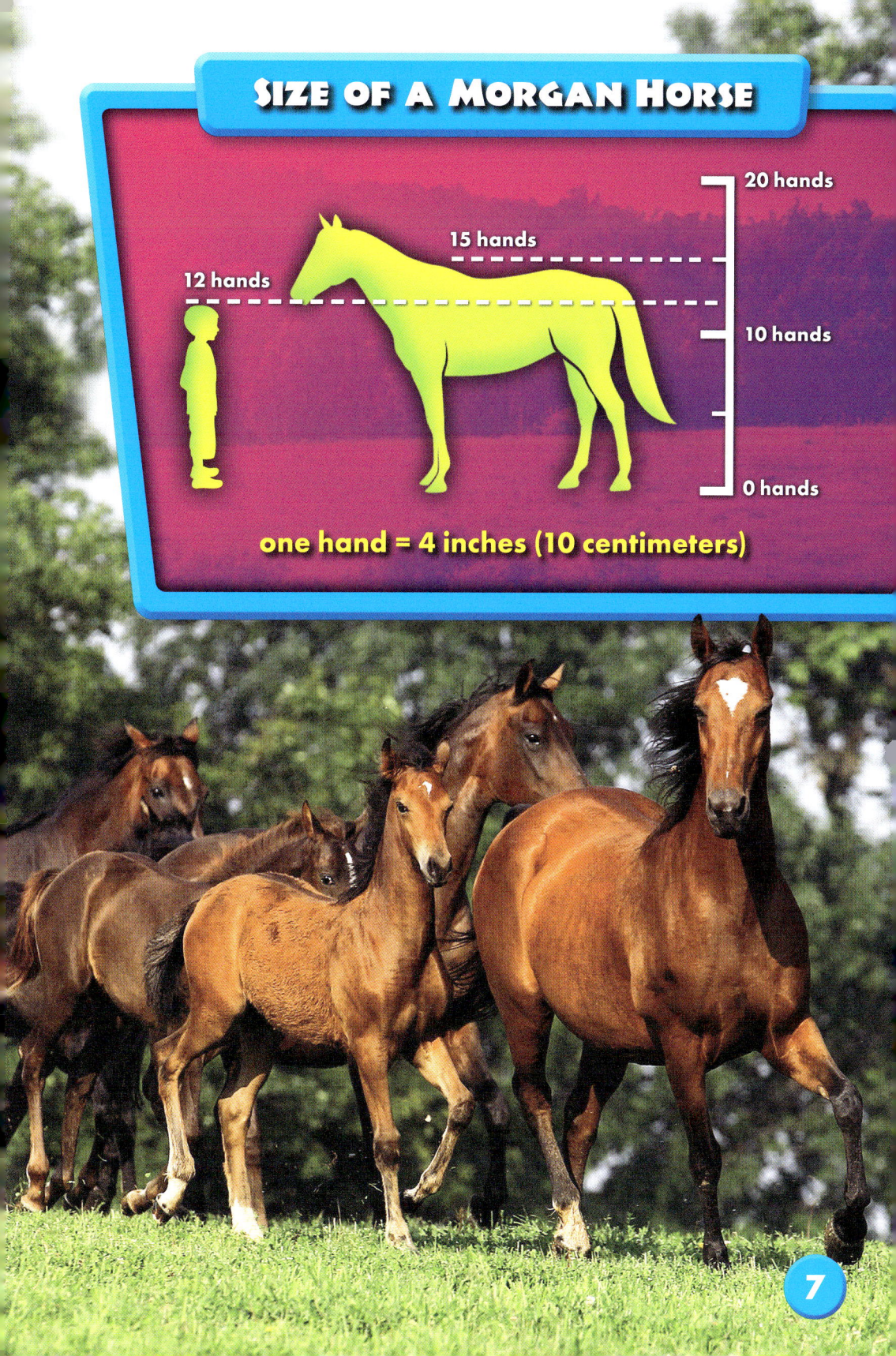

Morgan horses hold their heads and flowing tails high. These horses show off their big eyes and small ears.

mane

Thick **manes** hang from their curved necks.

bay coat

Morgan horses have different **coat** colors. **Bay** and **chestnut** coats are the most common.

Black coats are common, too.

COAT COLORS

bay

black

chestnut

Morgan Horse Beginnings

In 1789, a horse named Figure was born. He was very strong, fast, and kind.

In the 1790s, Justin Morgan became Figure's owner. They lived in Randolph, Vermont.

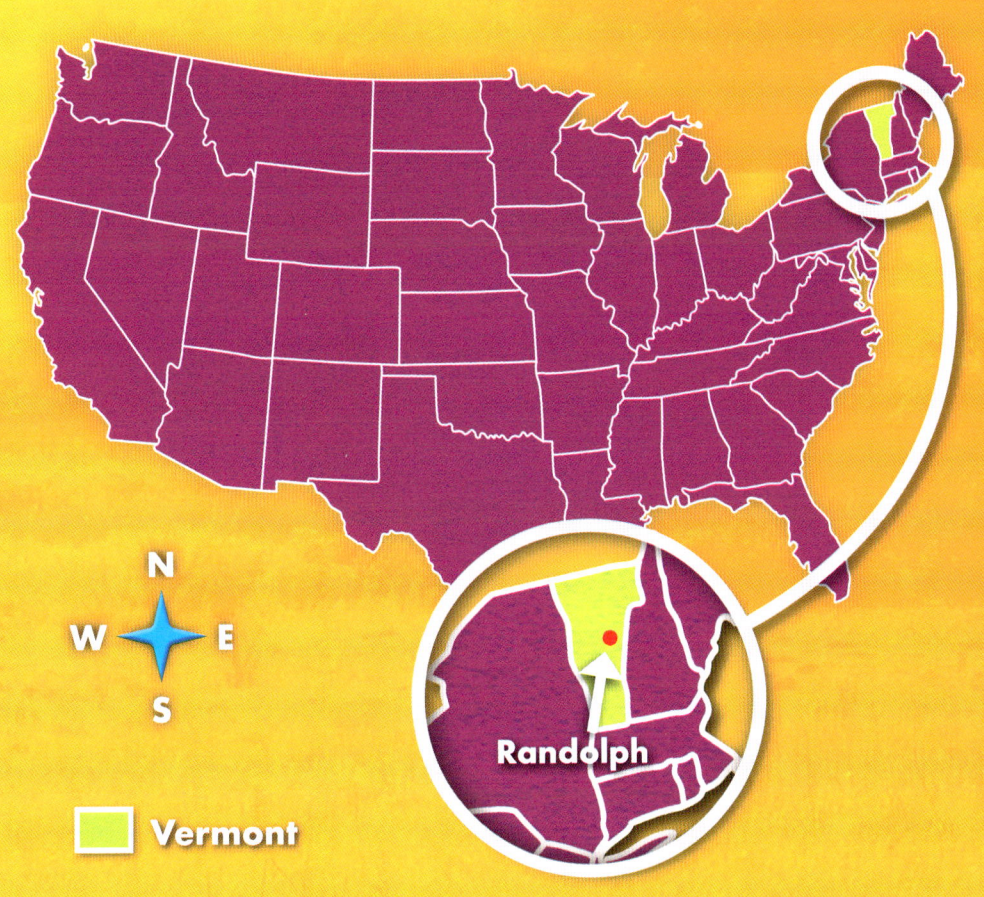

Justin Morgan **bred** Figure to pass on his outstanding **traits**. Figure's **colts** became the first Morgan horses!

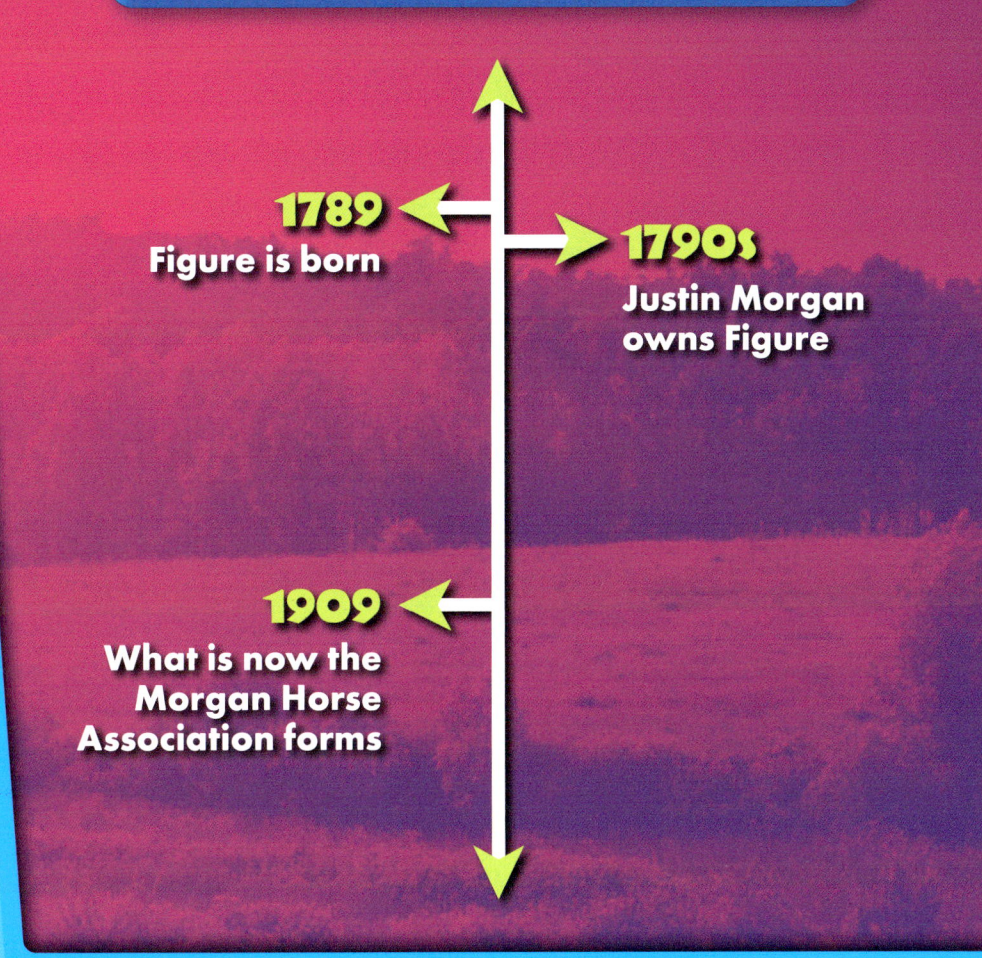

Morgan Horse Timeline

1789 Figure is born

1790s Justin Morgan owns Figure

1909 What is now the Morgan Horse Association forms

In 1909, owners formed what is now the Morgan Horse Association.

Talented Friends

Morgans have great **endurance**. They are tireless horses.

These hard workers can pull wagons and **plow** fields.

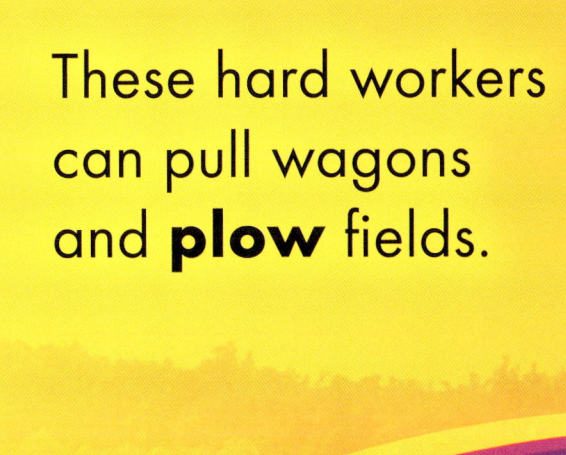

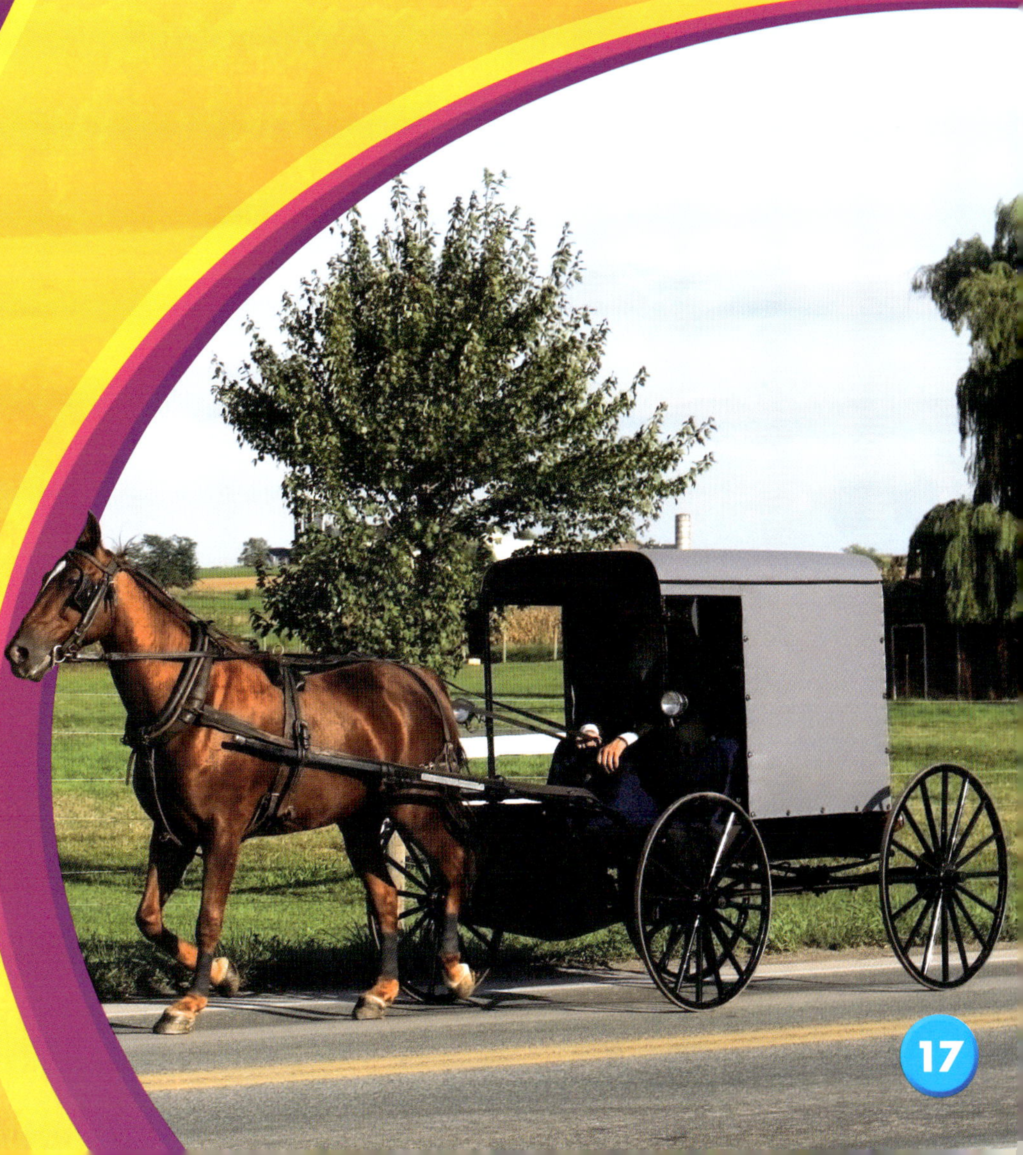

Morgan horses are **graceful** and easy to train. They are skilled in many events. Riders often choose them for jumping and **dressage**.

dressage

Horsing Around
Jumping

upright jump

square oxer

triple bar jump

Morgans love their owners. They quickly become friends with strangers, too. These calm horses can be wonderful **therapy animals**.

Morgan horses can win anyone's heart!

Glossary

bay—a coat color with a reddish-brown body and a black mane, ears, and tail

bred—purposely mated with other horses to make horses with certain qualities

breed—a certain type of horse

chestnut—a reddish-brown color

coat—the hair or fur covering some animals

colts—young male horses

dressage—a horse show event judged on movement, balance, and the ability to follow directions

endurance—the ability to keep going for a long time

graceful—related to smooth and beautiful movements

hands—the units used to measure the height of a horse; one hand is equal to 4 inches (10 centimeters).

manes—hair that grows from the necks of horses

plow—to turn over soil by pulling a piece of farm machinery called a plow

therapy animals—animals that comfort people who are sick, hurt, or have a disability

traits—qualities that make one horse different from the others

To Learn More

AT THE LIBRARY
Jazynka, Kitson. *Gallop! 100 Fun Facts About Horses.* Washington, D.C.: National Geographic, 2018.

Meister, Cari. *Morgan Horses.* Mankato, Minn.: Amicus, 2019.

Mills, Andrea. *The Everything Book of Horses & Ponies.* New York, N.Y.: DK Publishing, 2019.

ON THE WEB

FACTSURFER

Factsurfer.com gives you a safe, fun way to find more information.

1. Go to www.factsurfer.com.
2. Enter "Morgan horses" into the search box and click 🔍.
3. Select your book cover to see a list of related content.

Index

bred, 14
breed, 4
coat, 10, 11
colors, 10, 11
colts, 14
dressage, 18
ears, 8
endurance, 16
events, 18
eyes, 8
Figure, 12, 13, 14
heads, 8
jumping, 18, 19
manes, 9
Morgan, Justin, 13, 14
Morgan Horse
 Association, 15
necks, 9
plow, 17
pull, 6, 17
races, 4
Randolph, Vermont, 13
riders, 18
shows, 4
size, 6, 7
tails, 8
therapy animals, 20
timeline, 15
train, 18
traits, 14
work, 4, 17

The images in this book are reproduced through the courtesy of: Lisa Kolbenschlag, cover, pp. 16-17; Linda Richards/ Alamy, pp. 4-5, 18; Christopher Crosby Morris, pp. 5, 12-13, 14-15; Rosanne Tackaberry/ Alamy, p. 6; bob langrish/ Alamy, pp. 6-7; WILDLIFE GmbH/ Alamy, pp. 8-9; Panther Media GmbH/ Alamy, pp. 9, 11 (black); Juniors Bildarchiv GmbH/ Alamy, pp. 10-11; Melissa E Dockstader, p. 11 (bay); Bold Step, p. 11 (chestnut); Joy Brown, p. 17; ZUMA Press Inc/ Alamy, pp. 20-21; Donna Kilday/ Dreamstime, p. 21.